W9-AAR-328

LITTLE RUNNER

OF THE LONGHOUSE

LITTLE RUNNER

OF THE LONGHOUSE

LITTLE

An I CAN READ Book

RUNNER
OF THE LONGHOUSE

by BETTY BAKER
pictures by Arnold Lobel

HARPER & BROTHERS · PUBLISHERS

LITTLE RUNNER OF THE LONGHOUSE
Text Copyright © 1962 by Betty Baker Venturo
Pictures Copyright © by Arnold Lobel
Printed in the United States of America

All rights reserved. No part of the book may be used or reproduced in any manner whatsoever without written permission except in the case of brief quotations embodied in critical articles and reviews. For information address Harper & Brothers, 49 East 33rd Street, New York 16, N. Y.

Library of Congress catalog card number: 62-8040

for MEG

It was cold in the longhouse.

Little Runner jumped out of bed and ran to the fire.

He sat down
with his father
and Little Brother.
His mother gave them
something to eat.
Many other Indians
lived in the longhouse, too.
There was always a lot to do,
but everyone helped.

Little Runner helped, too.
And he knew there
was a special time
to do each thing.
There was a time
to make maple sugar.

And a time

to put away the corn.

There was a time

to go hunting.

And a time to trade

with other Indians.

But Little Runner thought
the best time was today.
This was the time
of the New Year.
Today there would be dances
and games to play
and a lot to eat.
Soon men came
to dance in the longhouse.

When the dances were over,

other men came

to tell stories.

Everyone sat by the fire

to hear them.

Then some big boys
came to the longhouse.
The boys wore old clothes
and funny masks.

An old woman was with them.

She had a big basket.

It was the biggest basket

Little Runner had ever seen.

The big boys

went to each family

in the longhouse.

Each family gave them something

to put in the big basket.

Mother gave the boys
some maple sugar.
They put the maple sugar
in the basket.
Then the boys did a dance
to say thank you.
"Mother," said Little Runner.
"Why did you give the boys
the maple sugar?"
Mother said,
"If I did not give them
something for the basket,
they would take something.

Maybe they would take

my new moccasins.

Or my cooking pot.

Then I would have to buy it back.

I would have to pay for it

with *much* maple sugar."

"Oh," said Little Runner.

"That is fun.

I want to go with the big boys."

"Not this New Year," said Mother.

"When you are a big boy

you can go

with the basket woman."

Little Runner thought about it.

Then he put on a mask

and ran to his mother.

"Ha!" he said.

"I am a big boy.

And I want maple sugar.

Much maple sugar.

Give me maple sugar

or I will take something."

"Oh, big boy," Mother said.

"What will you take?"

Little Runner said,

"I will take the new moccasins

and the cooking pot."

"But I will see you,"

Mother said.

"And if I see you take them,

you must put them back.

That is the way it is."

"Oh," said Little Runner.

He took off the mask.

Little Brother said,

"Come play in the snow,

Little Runner."

Little Runner took Little Brother

to play in the snow.

They played snow snake.

Little Brother

was not very good.

He was too little.

But Little Runner

could make his snake stick

go far in the snow.

Then Little Runner saw the big boys
going from longhouse to longhouse.
He thought about the boys
and the maple sugar.
He looked at Little Brother.
Then he laughed.

Little Runner went
into the longhouse
and put on his mask.
"I am a big boy," he said.
"And I have Little Brother.
You would not give me
much maple sugar.
So I took Little Brother.
Now you must buy him back."
"Ah," said Mother.
"What do you want
for Little Brother?"

"A canoe," said Little Runner.

"What will you do

with a canoe?" said Mother.

Little Runner said,

"I will take the canoe

down the river

to get shells

to make wampum

to trade for all the maple sugar

I can eat."

"No," Mother said.

"A canoe is too much.

You can keep Little Brother."

Little Runner looked about.

Then he said,

"Will you give me

the three deerskins

for Little Brother?"

"What will you do

with three deerskins?"

Mother asked.

Little Runner said,

"I will trade the three deerskins

for a canoe

to go down the river

to get shells

to make wampum

to trade for all the maple sugar

I can eat."

"No," Mother said.

"Three deerskins are too much.

You keep Little Brother."

Little Runner thought.

Then he said,

"Will you give me

the big bow and arrows

for Little Brother?"

"What will you do

with the big bow and arrows?"

Mother asked.

Little Runner said,

"I will take the big bow and arrows

and hunt for three deer

to make deerskins

to trade for a canoe

to go down the river

to get shells

to make wampum

to trade for all the maple sugar

I can eat."

"No," Mother said.

"The big bow and arrows

are too much.

You keep Little Brother."

Little Runner thought some more.
Then he said,
"Will you give me a good knife
for Little Brother?"
"What will you do
with a good knife?"
asked Mother.
Little Runner said,
"I will take the good knife
and make a big bow and arrows
to hunt three deer
to make deerskins
to trade for a canoe
to go down the river

to get shells

to make wampum

to trade for all the maple sugar

I can eat."

"No," Mother said.

"A good knife is too much.

But I will give you

a big bowl of maple sugar."

"I will take it,"

said Little Runner.

"Now you can have Little Brother."
Mother laughed and said,
"But I HAVE Little Brother.
He came into the longhouse
with you.
He is sitting by the fire."

Little Runner laughed, too.
Then he took off his mask
and sat by the fire
with Little Brother.
Mother gave them a big bowl.
It was full of maple sugar.
All the maple sugar
Little Runner and his brother
could eat.